We Are One

YSAYE M. BARNWELL

Illustrated by BRIAN PINKNEY

Harcourt, Inc. *Orlando Austin New York San Diego London*

www.HarcourtBooks.com

Library of Congress Cataloging-in-Publication Data
Barnwell, Ysaye M.
We are one/Ysaye M. Barnwell; illustrated by Brian Pinkney.
p. cm.
Summary: Illustrated text of the Sweet Honey
In The Rock song celebrating the unity of humankind.
1. Children's songs—Texts. [1. Songs.] I. Pinkney, Brian, ill.
II. Sweet Honey In The Rock (Musical group). III. Title.
PZ8.3.B25252Wer 2008
[782.42]—dc22 2006010225
ISBN 978-0-15-205735-0

First edition
A C E G H F D B

Printed in Singapore

The illustrations in this book were done in watercolor and gouache on Arches cold-pressed watercolor paper.
The calligraphy was created by Judythe Sieck.
Color separations by SC Graphic Technology Pte Ltd, Singapore
Printed and bound by Tien Wah Press, Singapore
Production supervision by Christine Witnik
Designed by April Ward

This book is dedicated to my ancestors, and yours,
because at this moment we are the whole reason they existed. . . .
And this book is dedicated to you, because you are creating the future

—Y. M. B.

To Liz, Lisa, and Paul

—B. P.

For each child that's born,
a morning star rises
and sings to the universe
who we are.

We are
our grandmothers'
prayers.

We are
our grandfathers'
dreamings.

We are
the breath of our ancestors.

We are
the spirit of God.

We are
Mothers of courage,

Fathers of time,

Daughters of dust,

Sons of great vision.

We are
Sisters of mercy,

Brothers of love,

Lovers of life and

the Builders of nations.

We are
Seekers of truth,

Keepers of faith,

Makers of peace and
the Wisdom of the ages.

We
Are One